DARK HANDS OF ANUBIS

A David Harris & Emma Jackson Mystery

BONUS EDITION

ANGELA VAN BREEMEN

Iconic Scribes Press Inc.

ISBN

978-1-0689909-8-4 (Paperback)

978-1-7383130-4-4 (eBook)

1.FICTION, Mystery & Detective / General

2.FICTION, Mystery & Detective / Amateur Sleuth 3. FICTION, Occult &Supernatural

Distributed to the trade by The Ingram Spark Company All rights reserved.

ANGELA VAN BREEMEN

Contents

Acknowledgements

I am grateful to author Peter Thomas Pontsa for his editorial suggestions. Thank you.

Finally, any errors or inconsistencies are my own, keep in mind that this book is a work of fiction and meant to entertain.

This short story provides background to the nefarious Dark Hands of Anubis, the secret organization which plays a huge role throughout the David Harris and Emma Jackson Mystery series. It is also a teaser for book 3 in the series.

I hope you will find this free giveaway enjoyable.

With humble thanks,

Angela van Breemen

One

Amelia's Fine Dining

David and Emma sat near the cozy fireplace at Amelia's Fine Dining, where they had enjoyed their first date over two years ago.

Summer had loosened its grip and was slowly giving way to the crisper temperatures of early fall with deep blue September skies, warm days and cool nights where the warmth of the hearth took off the chill.

Emma reached out and took David's hand, her thumb stroking the inside of his palm. "Thanks for suggesting we go out for dinner tonight," she said beaming. "I love it when we cook at home, but sometimes it's nice to be pampered. And Amelia's is my favourite restaurant."

Local historians said that the fine restaurant was named after Amelia Earhart who was believed to have frequented the establishment in 1918 when she became a nurse's aide in nearby Toronto. It was rumored that Niki Davros, the owner of the restaurant then known as Niki's, was so enamored by the feisty young woman that he renamed his restaurant, Amelia's Fine Dining. Several generations later, the restaurant continued to win awards and accolades from food critics worldwide.

Being a vegetarian, Emma's starter had been thinly sliced golden and red beets topped with whipped goat cheese, pistachio dust, and microgreens, and aged balsamic pearls. David had ordered Mussels à la crème de safran; Prince Edward Island mussels in a saffron cream broth with leeks, fennel, and a drizzle of chive oil.

The two had just finished and were waiting for their main entrées. "That was delicious," Emma said, balancing a long-stemmed wine glass in her hand. "I can't wait to try the mains. Every time we come here, it inspires me with new recipe ideas."

As elegant as she was, she was also earthy, her fingernails short, a practical solution to keeping her nails clean since she was a gardener. Her passion was growing herbs for her specialty teas. Her friend Megan, who identified as non-binary, was a barista at Café Mokka and Emma's blend of teas was now offered for sale at the small café.

"After the last case, we deserve some 'us' time," David said, his warm brown eyes gazing into hers. The firelight caught the highlights in Emma's auburn hair, causing it to shimmer and shine. His breath caught in his throat, "How did I get so lucky to have you in my life?"

Emma's cheeks turned slightly pink. "Ah, David, I feel the same." As she leaned forward, an unruly strand of hair escaped the loose chignon, and fell across her face. "As long as we're together, it's always wonderful, no matter what we do."

David reached across the table and tucked a tendril of wavy hair behind her ear. He was roughly six feet tall with a slim and athletic build and kept himself fit by rowing and lifting weights. Since meeting Emma he now practiced yoga regularly and joined her in meditation sessions to become more attuned with the spiritual world around him.

"You're so sweet to me." She gave him a contented smile, her eyes lighting up at his tender gesture. "This really is nice."

David's posture straightened, his eyebrows raising in surprise. "It can't be!"

"What is it?"

"I don't believe it!" David's tone was incredulous.

"Don't keep me in suspense! What is it?" she asked again.

"I think I just saw Reinhard." David motioned toward the window on his right.

"Are you sure? Reinhard is dead ... we saw him die." Her voice faltered.

"Yeah. I know but ..." He frowned. "Weird. It must have been the lighting."

"After what we've been through because of the Dark Hands of Anubis, it will take a while for things to feel normal again," said Emma, her intonation soft and reassuring.

David cleared his throat, and asked, "Do you sense anything?"

"Not really." She was reluctant to say that the only empathic impressions she was getting was her husband's rising panic.

"When that monster captured us and then separated you from me, it was agonizing."

A few months earlier, Reinhard Holtz (III), second-in-command of the sinister sect, the Dark Hands of Anubis, and great-grandson of the founder had been killed by Interpol. The team's investigation into the human-trafficking and baby ring business that had been cultivated by the nefarious organization took a turn for the worse when Megan and their nieces were kidnapped by Reinhard's henchmen.

During their investigation, David, Bryan and Emma learned that the young women had been taken to the mountains of Nicaragua where Reinhard conducted his operations from his luxury villa overlooking the Maribios mountain range. Below the villa he had concealed an underground compound and medical facility where young women were forced to breed made-to-order children for the ultra rich.

While on their rescue mission, David, Emma and Bryan had been captured during an ambush. Reinhard had taken a liking to Emma's striking looks and had brought her to his villa, while David and Bryan remained imprisoned in a shack further down the mountain.

"Those were terrible times," Emma said, shuddering at the thought of Reinhard. Tall and angular, with distinct Aryan features, he had been psychologically unstable and driven by a deep-seated sense of superiority that manifested in cruelty and ruthlessness. "But with the help of Spirit Anna and Maggie, we escaped. I doubt anyone who ever crossed his path is mourning his death."

Emma was referring to Anna Tungsten, a psychic and Emma's instructor, who, two years earlier, had been tortured and murdered by Enrico Bianchi to retrieve damning video evidence linking him to the murders of David's former self, Samuel Larson, and real estate businessman Chris Beacon.

From the spirit world, Spirit Anna had helped the team with their next case. Maggie, who had disappeared at the age of sixteen, and died in childbirth ten years later, was unable to move on to the afterlife. Spirit Anna had helped Emma develop her psychic abilities further and given Maggie the closure she needed to move on. But now, Spirit Anna was also moving on, encouraging Emma to work with her own Spirit Guides.

She took his hand again and held it tight. "It's over."

You're right," said David. "It's probably nothing,"

"Maybe." Emma hesitated. "After Reinhard's death in Nicaragua, we assumed that the Dark Hands of Anubis organization was harmed irreparably, or better yet, destroyed. But—"

"—What if we've made a terrible assumption?" David blurted out.

"I'm still not sensing anything," Emma said, pausing. "But I think you should call Bryan anyway."

Their conversation was interrupted by their server.

"Your dinner will be just a few more minutes," he said. "May I top up your glasses?"

"Yes, please," said Emma. The server filled Emma's glass, then turned toward David.

"And you, sir?" David gestured toward his wineglass which had hardly been touched, "No, I'm good for now. Thanks."

"Very good, sir. I'll be back with your entrées shortly."

When the server returned, Emma gasped with delight at her meal. The Truffle Risotto Carnaroli had been slowly cooked in mushroom broth, finished with shaved black truffle and Parmigiano-Reggiano crisps. "This is amazing," she said, savoring her first bite.

David's meal was equally stunning; he had gone with surf and turf; beef tenderloin, medium rare and a skewer of jumbo shrimp marinated in garlic. Mini roasted potatoes and asparagus in a crème sauce finished off the beautifully presented dinner.

"Your meal looks great, too," said Emma. "A walk in the gardens after dinner?" she asked, tucking into her dinner with enthusiasm. "It's a bit chilly, but I'd be interested to see what it looks like this time of year." Amelia's Fine Dining was famous for their beautiful "night" gardens located behind the establishment.

"Not sure." David leveled worried eyes at her, setting his knife and fork down. "Em, I've lost my appetite. Finish your meal and then if it's okay with you, I'd like to head home."

Emma put her utensil down. "How about we get our meals boxed up for us, then we can leave right away."

"You're not upset?"

"No, only worried that you are uneasy. Like I said, I'm not sensing any immediate danger ... but that doesn't mean that your instincts aren't right."

"Thanks, Em."

David motioned to the server. "Would you get us the bill, please?"

"Of course, sir, were your dinners not to your satisfaction?" the waiter asked, his forehead furrowing with concern.

"They were great," said David. "Something urgent has come up and we need to leave early. Do mind boxing up our meals up for us?" asked David.

"Most certainly, sir."

After the bill was settled, David and Emma walked to their car. Once seated in the Kia EVS, David engaged the vehicle's phone projection system and called Bryan Grant, his father-in-law and recently retired police officer from New Elgan Police Services.

Missing being on the force, Bryan now worked as a liaison officer for the police department and for their firm, Jackson, Grant & Harris Investigations. Their primary mandate was to work on solving cold cases using the paranormal, which is where Emma's skills came in to play, and good old-fashioned detective work which is where Bryan and David's skills were most valuable. Emma's mother, Laura, ensured their office ran smoothly.

"Hey, Bryan," said David.

"Hello, son. What are you doing calling on a Friday night? Thought it was date night with Emma." Bryan hesitated. "Is everything all right?"

"Not exactly." David cleared his throat. "Something's come up. Can you and Laura meet us at the office tomorrow morning?"

"Of course. What's going on?" asked Bryan.

"This is going to sound crazy but I thought I saw Reinhard Holtz outside the restaurant."

"But he's dead!" The shock is Bryan's voice was palpable. "I can see why you want to meet. Does ten o'clock work for you?"

"Sure thing. See you then."

David disconnected the call, checked his blind spot, pulled the car out of the parking lot, and said, "Let's head home."

Two

The Chase

On the bypass around downtown New Elgan, David squinted against the glare of high beams in his rearview mirror. "What a creep." He glanced away, blinking rapidly at the temporary spots and patterns impairing his vision.

"What is it?" asked Emma.

"Gotta tailgater. An SUV. Can't even see his license plate."

Curious, Emma swiveled in her seat to look back. "Wow, that's bright!" she said, shading her eyes with her right hand.

"This is ridiculous!" The Kia EV6 shot forward as David pressed on the accelerator of the electric vehicle, getting full force immediately. The Kia pulled away effortlessly.

"David, that was a bit too fast, don't you think?"

"Yeah, but the new Michelins are perfect. The tires are sticky and stay planted on the road making them especially great for quick acceleration."

David looked at the lights behind him fading in the distance. "We lost them," he said with relief, returning the vehicle back to the speed limit of 80 kilometers per hour.

"Not so sure about that," said Emma, turning to look over her shoulder. "Looks like they are coming up fast behind us." Seconds later, the vehicle was right behind them, high beams on, the bright halogen lights revealing Emma's frightened face.

"Yep, they've caught up to us." David's eyes narrowed with annoyance. "What's their problem?"

"David, I'm scared!" He heard her gasp. "They're practically in the back seat! Are they going to force us off the road?"

Seconds later the driver rammed their rear bumper, causing the Kia to swerve slightly to the right.

Emma's eyes widened in fright. "Oh my God!" Her fingers trembled as she fumbled through her purse for her phone.

"Sh—t!" David straightened the car before it hit the soft shoulder and accelerated again, causing Emma's phone to fly out of her fingers, and slip between the console and her seat.

Thank God for the NorthStar EV Racing School, he thought. He had recently taken an advanced driving course, knowing the EV6 had a lot of power under its hood, very different from a conventional engine.

David, a lawyer, was hardly used to high-speed car chases and was shocked at the situation in which he and Emma found themselves. Grateful for what he'd learned on the track, he pressed the accelerator again and shot forward, this time keeping his speed up. He threaded through the sluggish stream of traffic with practiced ease, the car behind him fading to a tiny speck of light before it blinked out.

David waited a few more seconds, then made a hard left onto a side street. He powered down the vehicle, turned off the exterior and interior lights manually, and waited.

"Is that them?" asked Emma, pointing at the rapidly moving car.

"Yeah, I believe so."

"You're going to follow them?" Emma's breath caught in her throat. "Shouldn't we call the police?" she asked, still trying to retrieve the cell phone where it remained stubbornly wedged.

"Let's see what they're up to," David said through clenched teeth, pulling back onto the road and keeping a discreet distance behind the SUV.

"David," said Emma. "I'm getting a message from Pieter, my guardian angel." She frowned, "and also from Frederick my gatekeeper. They say our pursuers are heading toward our house!"

As part of her psychic training, Emma had been encouraged by both Spirit Anna and her mother to work with Mona, a powerful psychic and empath. Although Spirit Anna had served as Emma's guide, she was moving on to do other spiritual work and wanted Emma to become in tune with her own guides.

Mona had explained that a person has at least three guides. A main guide, a guardian angel, and a gatekeeper and depending on what is going on in one's life, there can be more than three. Emma had learned that her main guide was Salma, her guardian angel was Pieter, her grandfather on her mother's side and that her gatekeeper was a fierce and protective spirit named Frederick.

"We need to rethink this," David said, pulling over. "They might've planted a tracker."

"David, don't you think we should call the police?"

"Not yet," was his curt reply.

Having trained for his private investigator's license he'd learned about scanning for bugs. He powered down the vehicle, popped open the hatch and retrieved the Wideband RF Spectrum Analyzer.

David carefully scanned the car with the device. The analyzer screen flickered with static.

"What's that hum?" asked Emma.

"That's just the car talking to itself," he muttered, sweeping the rear undercarriage of the vehicle. "Inverters, control modules ... standard EM noise. It'll quiet down once the system powers down." David was interrupted by a loud electronic beep. "Found it." The device was nestled within the rear bumper cavity near the telemetry antenna module.

"So, what do we do now?"

"Not sure. If we remove it, they'll know we did ..."

"... and if we leave it in place, they can trace us wherever we go," said Emma completing David's sentence. "On the other hand, they already know we're on to them because you lost them back there."

"True. But they don't know we've discovered the tracker. Besides all that, there's some protocol here," he said. "It's better if we leave it in place and photograph it."

"Now can we call the police?"

David said, "In a minute." He took out his cell phone and took numerous photos of the device from multiple angles. "It's even got a serial number. I'll text this over to Bryan and also Staff Inspector Carlo Carducci at the New Elgan Police Service."

"Finally," said Emma, impatient. "That might help us determine who is following us."

"Let's head home and see if we've got company."

"Why bother? My guides already say we do."

"Better to confirm that."

David put the car in gear and merged back onto the main road. The drizzle that had started minutes earlier now slicked the pavement, reflecting streetlights like molten gold.

"Careful," said Emma, gripping the edge of her seat as they rounded a curve. "It's slippery."

"I've got it," David replied, but just as he spoke, the car was jolted again, the high beams from the pursuing vehicle reflected in the rearview mirror. "Sh—t!". The tires lost traction on the wet pavement, and the Kia fishtailed for a few heart-stopping seconds before the tires dug into the soft shoulder.

David took his foot off the accelerator allowing the car came to a full stop before the tires became completely lodged in the mud.

The SUV cut in front of them and braked hard, coming to a dead stop in the middle of the road. Its taillights glowed red against the slick pavement.

"Jesus, that was close!" Emma gasped. "I thought they were ahead of us."

"I thought so, too. They must have circled back. After all, they are tracking us." He gave her a grim and worried look. "Your door locked?"

"Yeah."

David exhaled shakily, pulse racing. "Guess they're not finished toying with us."

"But what do they want?" asked Emma. Her pulse thudded so hard she could feel it in her ears.

"Not sure," he muttered, eyeing the vehicle parked in front of them. "They're not getting out of the car." He massaged the back of his neck, a sure sign he was getting a tension headache.

The abrupt stop had dislodged the cellphone enough, allowing Emma to pry her fingers around the device. She took several pictures of the SUV and said, "I was hoping to get a shot of their license plate, but they removed it."

David looked in the rearview mirror. Nothing but empty asphalt and the faint shimmer of rain — no hope for help from a good Samaritan or witness should they need help.

After a few heart-stopping seconds, the SUV pulled away, red taillights disappearing in the rainy night.

Emma drew in a sharp breath. "They're leaving."

"Em, I need to check the car. Make sure the rims aren't damaged. Lock the door behind me."

"But they're gone ..."

"Em, just do it."

"Sure. Please be careful."

A few seconds later, David got back in the car. "No damage that I can see."

"Thank God."

"Let's just get home."

He pulled back onto the road, both hands gripping the wheel, white-knuckled, the silence in the car, tense.

Ten minutes later, David pulled onto their street and drove slowly past their house and parked.

"Did you leave all those lights on in the house?" asked Emma.

"Nope, you know I didn't."

"Yeah, I guess I do. They're brazen," said Emma.

"Em, I don't think it's coincidence that this incident follows closely what I saw in the window at the restaurant."

"I think so, too. It's the Dark Hands of Anubis ... but how? Surely that organization died with Reinhard ..."

"You know deep down it didn't, don't you?" said David, his voice soft.

"It's highly possible." Distracted, she raked her fingers through her curly hair, causing her chignon to come undone. She untangled the untidy mess, rummaged in her purse, found a hairband and tied her hair back into a ponytail. "So, what's next?"

"I'll text Carlo again with what's going on. Maybe he can send a cruiser to check it out."

"Good plan. And then?"

"I was about to suggest we head to your mom and Bryan's place, but on second thought, it's probably not such a good idea."

"Agreed, too much of a chance they'd follow us there."

"How about we stay at the New Elgan Hotel tonight?" suggested David.

"We could park at the office and then head there on foot."

"Perfect. They won't think it's unusual for our vehicle to be parked there."

"Don't you think it's a bit weird?" Emma asked. "With the tracker in place they can trace our movements anywhere, so why bother chasing us?"

"I was thinking that, too. What's the point?"

"To intimidate us."

"Just let them try," said David, his tone grim.

He pulled the Kia into the parking space designated for Jackson, Grant & Harris Investigations and parked.

Emma's stomach growled.

"I'm sorry, Em. You're hungry, aren't you?" said David. "You never did get to finish your dinner."

"It's okay—we have our doggy bags," she said, grabbing the two boxed dinners from earlier that evening.

***

By the time they reached the New Elgan Hotel, the adrenaline had begun to ebb, leaving exhaustion in its place. Safe now and settled on the couch in their hotel room with bellies full, the couple finally relaxed.

"Not the kind of romantic evening I meant for us," David said.

"I know, David. It's not your fault." Emma drew in a shaky breath, then released it slowly. "God, that was terrifying."

She placed her half-empty glass of red wine on the coffee table, yawned, then leaned against David. But even as she drifted against David's shoulder, she couldn't shake the feeling that someone or something was still watching.

He pulled her close, stroked her hair gently and asked, "How about we head to bed?"

"Not a bad idea. I really am tired," she said, rubbing at her eyes.

"After a good night's rest, you'll feel better," said David, stifling a yawn of his own. "Hopefully we can come up with a game plan when we meet with Bryan, Laura and Carlo."

"I hope so."

Three

The Dream

David was awakened abruptly by the sound of Emma's sobs. The digital clock on the hotel nightstand displayed two in the morning.

"Emma," he said, turning on the light. He touched her shoulder gently. "Wake up honey."

Emma's eyes slowly came back into focus. "David? I had that dream again."

"The one about that couple being murdered?"

"Yes," she said. "These dreams. They're getting worse. More detailed."

"Wait a second," said David. "Let me get you a brandy." He went to the hotel's bar fridge, pulled out one of the miniature bottles and poured its contents into a glass. "Drink this. It will steady your nerves."

"Thanks. You take such good care of me." Emma smiled through her tears. "God, I miss Spirit Anna."

"I understand, but you've made great progress working with your own guides."

"I know. You're right. It's just harder now."

"It won't stay that way. Your skills are still developing."

"The message was clearer this time: Our daughter is innocent. Save Thelma Tang." Emma sighed heavily. "That name. Thelma Tang. It rings a bell, but I can't quite place it."

"Me, too. How about we take a look?" He grabbed his iPhone, which was resting on the nightstand, pressed down on the side button of the device and commanded, "Siri, provide me all the information you have on Thelma Tang."

Seconds later, Siri answered. Thelma Tang was a seventeen-year-old girl who was tried in an adult court for the murder of her parents Alice and Albert Tang. Although the murder weapon was never found, circumstantial evidence indicated she was the murderer. The most compelling evidence was that Ms. Tang had chatted on social media platforms about her desire to gut and kill her parents. From the moment the charges were laid, Ms. Tang maintained that she was innocent and pled not guilty. She claims that she was framed, that she didn't use social media and that in fact someone had impersonated her, creating social media accounts. Tang was sentenced in 2024 to life in prison with no chance of parole for 25 years, for the first-degree murders of her parents in 2020. Despite two subsequent appeals, Ms. Tang remains incarcerated in the Grand Valley Institution for Women, the single federal women's prison in Ontario. Ms. Tang was quoted as saying, "I miss my parents. Not a day goes by that I don't think of them. I could never hurt them. And worse for me, is knowing that the killer is still at large."

"Wow, that poor family," said Emma, shuddering.

"No kidding. So, what do you think?" asked David. "Is this our next cold case?"

"Yeah, I think it might be. Except I'm worried about what happened at the restaurant and afterward with the car chase." She pulled the blankets up under her chin, yawning.

"It's still early. We should go back to sleep," said David.

"There's no reason to think this, but I can't help thinking the Dark Hands of Anubis has something to do with the death of Thelma's parents."

"We'll talk about all of this tomorrow with Bryan and Carlo. Try to rest now."

"G'night, David. I love you."

"Sweet dreams, sweetheart." David pulled Emma toward him, wrapped his body around her in a protective cocoon and nestled his face into her hair, breathing in the scent of lavender.

Secure and safe in his arms, Emma was soon asleep, her inhalations and exhalations as gentle as a soft summer breeze.

Four

Jackson, Grant & Harris Investigations

In the boardroom of Jackson, Grant & Harris Investigations, Bryan Grant leaned back in his chair. Laura sat beside him, while Emma and David faced them across the polished oak table.

Bryan was of medium height with gray eyes that were as solemn as those of a funeral director. He was sixty-five years of age, still strong, with an agile and perceptive mind. Last year, he'd retired from the New Elgan Police Service but was rehired as a civilian employee. No longer a sworn constable, he now served as a Cold Case Analyst / Investigator and Liaison Officer between the police and Jackson, Grant & Harris Investigations.

Laura and Bryan had met two years earlier when Emma and David had reached out to Inspector Grant to solve a thirty-year-old cold case — the death of Samuel Larsen, nearly thirty years earlier.

Together, Bryan, David, Emma and Laura now ran the Jackson, Grant & Harris Investigations. Laura was also Bryan's wife and handled their administration. David held his private investigator's license and was a lawyer, while Emma, using her psychic and empathic abilities, aided with their investigations into cold cases comprising missing persons and murders.

"I called Carlo," said Bryan, glancing at his wristwatch. "He should be here any minute."

"Ah, that explains the spread," said Emma, smiling. Everyone knew Carlo's weakness for espresso and biscotti.

As if on cue, the staff inspector breezed into the conference room. In his mid-forties, Carlo was of Mediterranean descent with animated dark eyes and thick wavy brown hair interspersed with streaks of slate grey. His mother's family was from Northern Greece and emigrated to Canada in the mid-1950s, while his father was from Florence.

His eyes brightened at the sight of the espresso machine and biscotti. "Thank you, Bryan," he said, gesturing toward the espresso machine, delicate demitasse cups and saucers and the tin of imported biscotti di Prato; the type you'd usually find in Florence. The twice-baked almond biscuits were dry and crunchy, perfect alongside coffee.

"It's our pleasure," said Bryan, beaming.

Over espressos, Carlo said, "I got your text, but it will take time to trace down the serial number of the tracking device. If we are successful at all."

"How come?" asked Emma, frowning.

"We face a number of issues. If it was bought with cash, sold anonymously, or drop-shipped under fake details, the serial number won't get us far."

"Oh, that's disappointing," said David.

"It's more complicated than that. Even if we traced the manufacturer of the device, we have to follow the legal process by getting a warrant or subpoenas to compel carriers or manufacturers to hand over subscriber or account information. That takes time and may be blocked by foreign providers or privacy laws."

"So, this is likely a dead end," said David, trying to keep his disappointment in check.

"Probably," Carlo admitted, swirling his espresso. "These things take time. Nothing happens overnight." Carlo took a sip of his espresso, savoring the rich coffee. "Che buono!" "How good!"

Laura smiled at the compliment. "Grazie." Youthful in appearance, Laura looked more like Emma's older sister than her mother. She was delicate and graceful, with a vivaciousness indicating a free spirit. Her emerald eyes were as lovely as her daughter's and her dark auburn hair was pulled into a tight bun in an attempt to tame the wild curls. It was the expressive eyebrows and smile, however, that made their family resemblance unmistakable.

"The device by itself is inconclusive, but we will make an attempt to trace its origin. David, you did do the right thing leaving the device in place."

"Thanks, do we still leave it there?"

"Where is your car parked now?"

"Here in the lot."

"Good. Leave it there. I'll send George Parker, our Digital Forensics Investigator, to examine the tracking device, then remove it for further analysis at the lab."

"We can have the car back tonight?" asked David.

"Of course. So, your text was sparse. Can you give me a bit more detail about what transpired last night?"

David proceeded to tell Carlo and the others about the night before. How he'd seen someone who looked like Reinhard Holtz peer at him through the window, and then the strange car chase where they were forced off the road and then seeing all the lights on in their house.

"Emma took pictures. The license plate was removed, but maybe the department can identify the type of vehicle?"

"That was smart. Emma, could you airdrop them to me?" asked Carlo.

"Already done," said Emma, giving him a tired smile.

"We were so uneasy by then, we decided to stay the night at the New Elgan Hotel and deal with everything in the morning," said David.

"That was a wise decision," said Carlo. He took another sip of the espresso, a momentary delight flashed across his face before he became serious again. "After you texted the image of the device, we did send a cruiser to your house," said Carlo. "But the house lights were off, everything looked in order. Nothing seemed suspicious to my officer."

"Thanks for doing that," said David. "I had a feeling they'd be gone by the time you got there."

Emma spoke up. "And there's the dream I had last night."

"Yes?" said Bryan. "A vision?"

"No, just a very powerful dream with a message about a couple that were murdered and some girl named Thelma."

"I remember that case," said Carlo. "Thelma Tang at age seventeen was tried as an adult for killing her parents, Alice and Albert Tang. Kid never wavered from her story. Insisted she was innocent."

"I think she might be," said Emma, her voice quiet.

"Well, at this point I doubt it has anything to do with the Dark Hands of Anubis. Besides the Tang case was closed," said Bryan, "and the girl convicted."

"I know, it's just that I can't help feeling there's more to it. Possibly still related to the Dark Hands, although I have no reason to think so."

"Working on cold cases is really our mandate. Not reopening old ones that were already solved," said Bryan.

"I guess you're right," said Emma, disappointed.

Bryan noticed her dismay. "Carlo, maybe you could let us review the Tang files, just in case there's something to Emma's psychic message?"

"Sure, you never know." Carlo turned toward Emma and said, "Anna Tungsten had similar insight. Her track record was solid and she was a legend in our department. I'll get the files."

Emma let out a sigh of relief. "Thank you."

"Bryan, you asked for more information on the Dark Hands of Anubis and our friends at the RCMP branch of Interpol have shared additional information with the department. We've prepared a dossier," Carlo said, handing the file to Bryan.

Carlo continued, "David, your instincts may be correct: the organization did not end with the death of Reinhard. There is reason to believe that it continues to flourish and has reinvented itself."

David, Emma and Laura got up from their chairs and crowded in behind Bryan, peering over Bryan's shoulder, while Carlo remained seated, a slight smile tugging at his lips as he pressed the button on the coffee machine to make another espresso.

Five

The File

TOP SECRET

CRIMINAL INTELLIGENCE REPORT (CIR)

CLASSIFICATION: NEPS CONFIDENTIAL / EYES ONLY
CASE REF: CIR-2025-47-DHA
DATE/TIME (UTC): 2025-09-18 18:40 |
SUBJECT: Dark Hands of Anubis — Transnational Child-Trafficking & Cult Activity
ORIGINATING UNIT: Major Crime / Intelligence Division
CASE LEAD: Det. Insp. Carlo Carducci

INTELLIGENCE SUMMARY:
The Dark Hands of Anubis (DHA) is a clandestine transnational organization operating under corporate fronts tied to the Holtz Foundation, Frankfurt. Evidence collected over eight months links DHA to child trafficking, ritual abductions, and illicit antiquities funding. Operations span Canada, Germany, Nicaragua, and Egypt, functioning through layered legal entities masking criminal activity.

THREAT ASSESSMENT

Category	Risk Level	Notes
Human Trafficking	Severe	Multinational coordination and concealment.
Financial / Political Influence	High	Corporate infiltration at executive level.
Violent / Ritual Activity	Elevated	Symbolic executions, occult undertones.
Intelligence Counteraction	Critical	Active obfuscation, cyber interference.

MODERN OPERATIONS

Corporate Fronts: Holtz Enterprises, Helios Biomedical Group, multiple shell firms.
Primary Crimes: Human trafficking, forced adoptions, biomedical experimentation, disinformation, antiquities theft.
Motto: "Through death comes control, and through secrecy comes salvation."

The creed merges Nazi pseudo-science with Egyptian ritual, framing victims as vessels of domination.

THE HOLTZ DYNASTY

Name	Role	Status
Reinhard Holtz Sr. Founder	Ex-SS operative; fused Nazi ideology with Egyptian mysticism.	Deceased
Frank Holtz* (66) (2nd generation)	CEO, Holtz Enterprises	Controls global holdings; maintains cult doctrine covertly.
Reinhard Holtz III (33) (father Frank Holtz) 3rd generation	Ran "baby-mill" reproduction programs (Canada and Nicaragua).	Deceased June 1st, 2025
Marian Holtz* (33)	CFO, Holtz Enterprises	Global affairs
Vivian Holtz* (28)	Marketing Director, Holtz Enterprises	International Sales
Frank Jr. (25)	Bachelor of Arts (B.A.) in Archaeology / Ancient Civilizations, Master of Arts in Egyptology, Ludwig-Maximilians-Universität München with top honors.	Whereabouts unknown since 2022.

* Public faces of "legitimate" business divisions.

PRIMARY LOCATIONS:

Ontario (Canada) Pier 1, South Simcoe Bay – warehouse hub Active
Hamburg (Germany) Nordstern Freight AG – shipping front Active
Nicaragua Biomedical facility, led by Reinhard Holtz III (deceased) Dismantled
Luxor (Egypt) Archaeological - export shell Active/Monitored

CONCLUSION

The Dark Hands of Anubis represent a modern hybrid of ideological extremism and organized crime. Descended from Nazi intelligence networks, the Holtz dynasty has transformed wartime profiteering into a global apparatus blending mysticism, science, and power. Their influence extends across borders and sectors, unified by a single tenet: Secrecy is power — and power demands control.

Silence filled the room as Bryan and the rest of the team read through the file.

"I'm astonished at the depth and breadth of the document," said Bryan. "Thank you for procuring this, Carlo."

"Glad to have been of help."

"So, Reinhard had siblings," Emma said. "Do you think they're after us because..."

David put a protective arm around his wife. "Yes, I think this may be about avenging Reinhard's death."

"The dossier has sparse details on the youngest grandson, Frank Junior. Just his age and that he graduated with top honors from the prestigious Ludwig-Maximilians-Universität München with a Masters of Arts in Egyptology," said Laura. "He was twenty-two when he graduated, but that was three years ago."

"But where has he been all this time?" asked Emma. "And is he here in New Elgan now?" She gave an involuntary shudder.

"We should try and find out." Carlo stroked his chin. "I can reach out to Interpol and ask if they can trace his movements," he said. "See if we can get more background information that will indicate where he's been these last few years."

"Do they at least have a picture of him?" asked Laura.

Bryan shuffled through the file, "A few pictures of his father, Frank Holtz, and his sisters, but nothing on Frank Junior."

"Those photos are really blurry," commented Emma. "Not much help."

Bryan looked at Carlo. "Can your contacts at Interpol get photos of the youngest son? Maybe better ones of the whole family?"

"Possibly."

"Let me see if I can find something online," said Emma, thumbing through her iPad. "Got something on the Holtz Enterprises website. Two sisters, Marian and Vivian. Pretty girls—both are blondes, blue-eyed." She scanned the page, frowning. "But no mention of Frank Junior."

Scrolling further, she paused. "Here's a pic of their dad, Frank Senior, though." She expanded the image with her index finger and thumb, displaying a haughty-looking man with lips drawn in a severe line, dressed in a corporate business suit.

"Uncanny," said David. "Spitting image of Reinhard. Only older."

"What are the odds?" asked Emma.

"Strong, I'd say," said Bryan. "The person David saw last night through the window at Amelia's may very well be Frank Holtz, Junior."

"What do we do next?" Emma asked, her voice trembling slightly.

Bryan closed the file, the soft thud echoing in the quiet room. He looked up. "Well," he said, his tone resolute, "if we want to get to the bottom of this, we'd better get operational."

Message from the Author

Dear Reader,

Thank you for reading my book. I highly value your opinion! Please consider leaving a review on Amazon.

Your feedback helps other readers discover this book. Visit the book's page on Amazon, and click "Write a customer review," and share your thoughts.

https://www.amazon.com/gp/product/B0FBFFH22W

or if you prefer, visit the QR link here and scan using your smartphone:

Your review makes a meaningful impact.

Thank you for your time and support!

Best regards,

Angela van Breemen

About the author

Angela van Breemen is the author of the David Harris and Emma Jackson Mystery Series. She is currently at work on the third installment, Revenge Not Taken Lightly.

An avid writer of poetry, Angela is a member of the Wordsmiths Writers' Group based in New Tecumseth, Ontario. She also belongs to the Crime Writers of Canada, the South Simcoe Arts Council, and The Writers' Union of Canada.

In addition to writing, Angela is a soprano soloist and a passionate advocate for her community. She frequently performs at charitable events and fundraisers, blending her love of music with her commitment to giving back.

Music and poetry have long been integral to her creative life. In early 2024, she released her debut album, In The Breeze—a Celtic-inspired collection featuring three original pieces based on her own poetry.

Angela is also a dedicated volunteer at the Procyon Wildlife Rehabilitation and Education Centre, an organization devoted to rescuing, rehabilitating, and safely releasing orphaned and injured Ontario wildlife.

She lives in Loretto, Ontario, with her husband, Peter Thomas Pontsa, author of the Inspector William Fox Series.

You can connect with Angela on:

https://angelavanbreemen.ca

https://www.facebook.com/angela.vanbreemen.5

https://www.instagram.com/stories/angelapearl55/

https://x.com/breemenangela

https://wildsongbird.ca

Subscribe to her newsletter: https://angelavanbreemen.ca/contact-us

Also by Angela van Breemen

Revenge is Not Enough: A David Harris and Emma Jackson Mystery –
Book Two.
http://books2read.com/revengeisnotenough
Past Life's Revenge: A David Harris and Emma Jackson Mystery – Book
One.
http://books2read.com/pastlifesrevenge
Whispering in the Dancing Wind – a poetry collection
https://www.amazon.ca/dp/B0FXHJMRGN

www.ingramcontent.com/pod-product-compliance
Lightning Source LLC
Chambersburg PA
CBHW032114170626
46808CB00008B/3051